I0765550

Hug a crab.

How to read this book

emotional support bird

This book has some
hard words.

The first time you see a
hard word

- the hard word is blue
- then you will see what the
hard word means.

bold

not bold

Names are written in **bold**.

How to read this book

The pictures help you understand the words.

You can ask for help to read this story from

- a friend
- family
- or a support worker.

Hug a crab

by **Casey Gray**

Meet **Fred**

This bird is called **Fred**.

Fred is **Eddy's** emotional support bird.

This emotional support bird helps **Eddy** feel better.

Meet **Fred**

Fred says things **Eddy** is thinking.

Fred says rude things to people like

- bad support workers
- bad group homes
- bad times with the NDIS
- bad doctors.

Meet **Fred**

Keep reading if you are ready for **Fred's** rude words.

Stop reading if you do not like rude words.

Fred is very rude.

Balls.

Lick my balls.

Backwards.

Bend over.

Bowling?

Shoot me.

Have a medal.

Wipe my ass.

Cupcake.

Prayers?

Yawn.

Bite me.

Bitch.

Vagina.

Chicken legs.

Penis.

Head.

Penis head.

Shit.

Bull.

Shit.

Bull shit.

Hug a crab.

Butt lips.

Honey?

Chicken?

Turkey neck.

Good person?

Yes Mum.

No.

You wait.

No.

No.

No.

No.

No.

No.

Sit on a cactus.

Sit and spin.

Up Uranus.

Up up up.

Look in the mirror.

Ciggy butt brain is **Fred's** name for support workers who make people wait while they take smoke breaks.

Burn baby.

Burn.

Eddy and their emotional support bird Fred

14 February 2025

Fun fact

In this book **Fred** can only use common words found on an AAC board.

AAC means Augmentative and Alternative Communication.

An AAC board helps people talk using pictures, symbols and sometimes words or letters.

Imagine kicking your toe but not having swear words on your AAC board.

Swearing helps with pain so how else could you express it?

You would need to get creative with the words and pictures you have.

AAC symbols that could be code for 'idea'

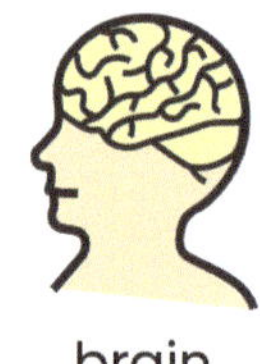

A page to say thank you

Thank you **Belinda** for inspiring me to write this story based on your bird that says rude words.

Thank you **Ben** and **Andie** for holding me accountable for writing this book.

Thank you **Bec** for being a supportive supporter.

Thank you to **Karen** and the other people who tested this book to see if it is easy and fun to read.

Printing information

Title: **Hug a crab**

Author: **Casey Gray**

Published by **Books By ED**

Copyright © 2025 **Casey Gray, Books By ED**

Images copyright © 2025 **Casey Gray.** Any stock images are used under license.

Symbols from **Mulberry Symbols** https://mulberrysymbols.org/ Copyright 2018/19 **Steve Lee** - This work is licensed under the Creative Commons Attribution-ShareAlike 2.0 UK: England & Wales License.

ISBN: 978-0-6459693-5-1

Books By ED, Gosford NSW, Australia.

All rights reserved. Set in Large Print minimum 14 pt. Poppins.

No part of this book may be reproduced or transmitted in any form or by any means, electronic or mechanical, including photocopying, recording, or by any information storage and retrieval system, without written permission from the author.

For more information https://www.byed.com.au/contact